WEEPING WILLOW

grief

MEZEREON

desire to please

HAWTHORNE

hope

MUSTARD SEED

indifference

CROW FOOT

ingratitude

BLUE VALERIAN

rupture

LILY OF THE VALLEY

return of happiness

BALM
sympathy

HAZEL

reconciliation

DAISY

I share your sentiments

LILAC

first emotions of love

ROSE

love

AMBROSIA

love returned

THE GREAT SMELLY, SLOBBERY, SMALL-TOOTH DOG

A FOLKTALE FROM GREAT BRITAIN

RETOLD BY MARGARET READ MACDONALD
ILLUSTRATED BY JULIE PASCHKIS

AUGUST HOUSE
Little folk
ATLANTA

For Ben of Rotterdam . . . who flung his slobber into this tale.

And for all those librarians . . . Rotterdam and beyond . . .
who have hosted me and my stories. Thanks for your company. —MRM

For Deborah Mersky and Jake. —JP

ABOUT THE STORY:

This tale is retold from *A Dictionary of British Folk-Tales* by Katharine M. Briggs
(Bloomington: Indiana University Press, 1970). It may remind you of another
story you have heard: "Beauty and the Beast." Folklorists call this Type 425C (Motif
B640) and have collected versions from around the world. Betsy Hearne compiled
a whole book full of these stories: *Beauties and Beasts* (Phoenix: Oryx Press, 1993).

Text copyright © 2007 by Margaret Read MacDonald.
Illustrations copyright © 2007 by Julie Paschkis.

Published 2007 by August House LittleFolk · www.augusthouse.com
3500 Piedmont Road NE, Suite 310 · Atlanta, Georgia 30305 · 404-442-4420

Illustrations are Windsor Newton gouache on Arches paper.
The text is set in Olduvai. Book design by Joy Freeman.
Manufactured in Korea. 10 9 8 7 6 5 4 3 2 1

LIBRARY OF CONGRESS CATALOGING-IN-PUBLICATION DATA
MacDonald, Margaret Read, 1940–
   The great smelly, slobbery, small-tooth dog : a folktale from Great Britain / retold by Margaret Read
MacDonald ; illustrated by Julie Paschkis.
      p. cm.
   Summary: In this British variant of a traditional tale, a great smelly, slobbery, small-tooth dog rescues
a rich man from bandits and demands that the man bring his beautiful daughter to live in his castle.
   ISBN 978-0-87483-808-4 (hardcover : alk. paper)
   [1. Dogs—Folklore. 2. Folklore—Great Britain.] I. Paschkis, Julie, ill. II. Title.

PZ8.M1755Gr 2007
398.2—dc22
[E]
                                                                                          2007005504

AUGUST HOUSE   PUBLISHERS   ATLANTA

A rich man was set upon by thieves.

But suddenly a
GREAT SMELLY, SLOBBERY, SMALL-TOOTH DOG
leaped from the bushes.

"WOOF!"

The dog chased the robbers away.

"You saved my life," said the man.

"Come to my house tomorrow.
I will give you one of my treasures.

"In my house I have a golden fish that can speak one hundred languages. Would you like that fish as your reward?"

"NO," said the dog. "I would not."

"In my house I have a golden bird that can sing one thousand songs. Would you like that bird?"

"NO! I would not."

"I also have a golden goose. It lays one egg a day. Solid gold. Would you like that?"

"NO! I would not."

"I have named all my treasures. What could you want?"

"In your house you have . . . a beautiful daughter!
That is the treasure I choose!"

It was true, the man's daughter
was his greatest treasure,
but he hadn't thought about that.
"Come to my house tomorrow," he said sadly.

So the man had to go home and tell his daughter all that had happened.

But his daughter was not afraid.

"You gave your word," she said. "I will go with the
GREAT SMELLY, SLOBBERY, SMALL-TOOTH DOG."

Next day the dog came to take her away.

"Jump onto my back!
Hold tight to my fur.
I'll take you to my house!
You're going to *like* it there."

She climbed onto his back
and held tight to his fur.

Off he ran . . . over the fields . . . to the first hedge.
And he LEAPED that hedge in a single bound.

And over the fields . . . to the second hedge.
And he LEAPED that hedge in a single bound.

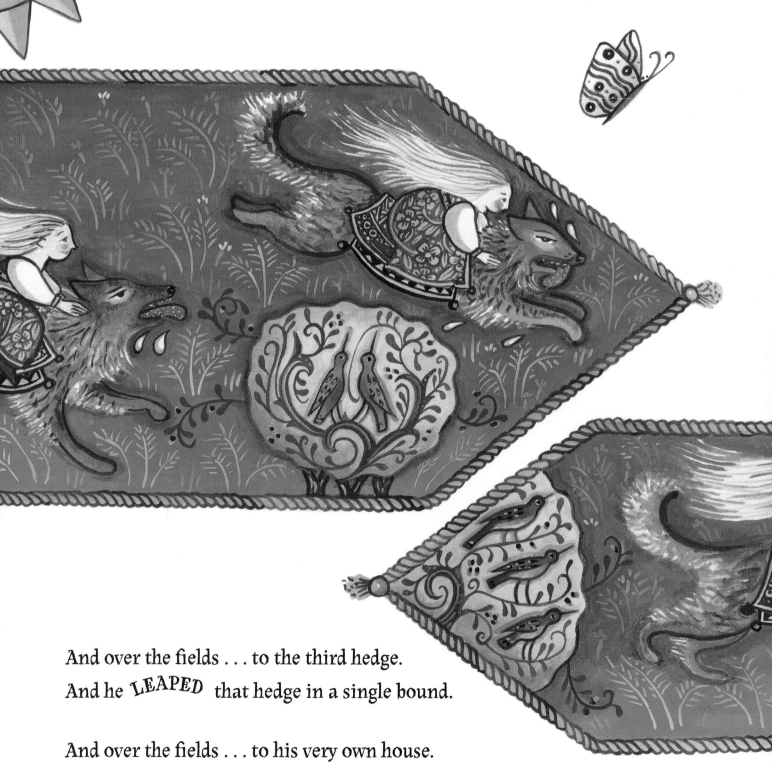

And over the fields . . . to the third hedge.
And he LEAPED that hedge in a single bound.

And over the fields . . . to his very own house.

His house was a *castle*!

There was a bed with silken sheets,
        a closet of silk and satin dresses in just her size,

and shelves of books—
just the kind she liked to read.

Every evening the dog came to her room to dine.
And after dinner he told her such funny stories . . .
she laughed and laughed.

In the afternoons they would play on the lawn.
She would throw his golden ball . . . and he would bring it back.
She would throw the ball again . . . and he would bring it back.

Then they would sit in the shade of a tree and
he would lay his great head in her lap.
She would stroke his soft fur,
even though it was smelly,
and murmur . . .

"Dear Dog, you are SWEET AS A HONEYCOMB!
As SWEET AS A HONEYCOMB!"

But at night when she was alone in her room,
she would think of her father
and miss him so.

"I'm held prisoner here by a
GREAT SMELLY, SLOBBERY, SMALL-TOOTH DOG!"

One day the dog found her weeping.

"What is wrong?
Don't I give you everything to make you happy?"

"Every *thing*, yes, but I miss my father!"

"I'll take you home for a visit.
Climb onto my back and
I will take you there."

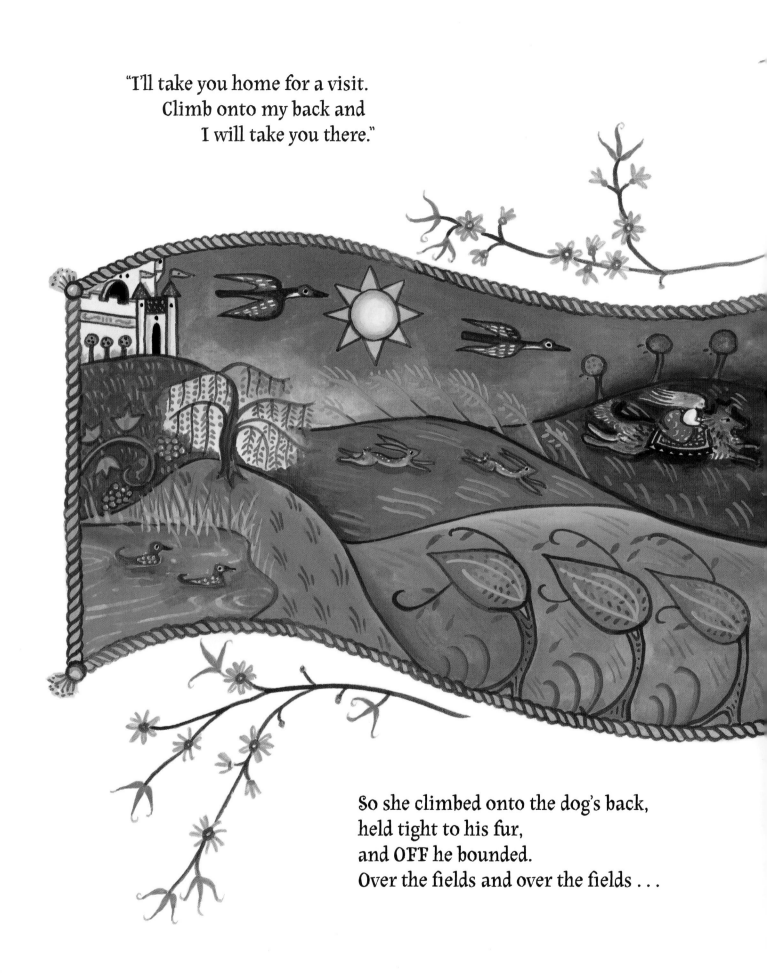

So she climbed onto the dog's back,
held tight to his fur,
and OFF he bounded.
Over the fields and over the fields . . .

But when he came to the first hedge he stopped.
"Wait. What's that you always call me?"

She knew what he wanted to hear.
"I call you SWEET AS A HONEYCOMB."

"YES!" He LEAPED the hedge in a single bound.
And over the fields . . . to the second hedge.

"What's that you call me?"

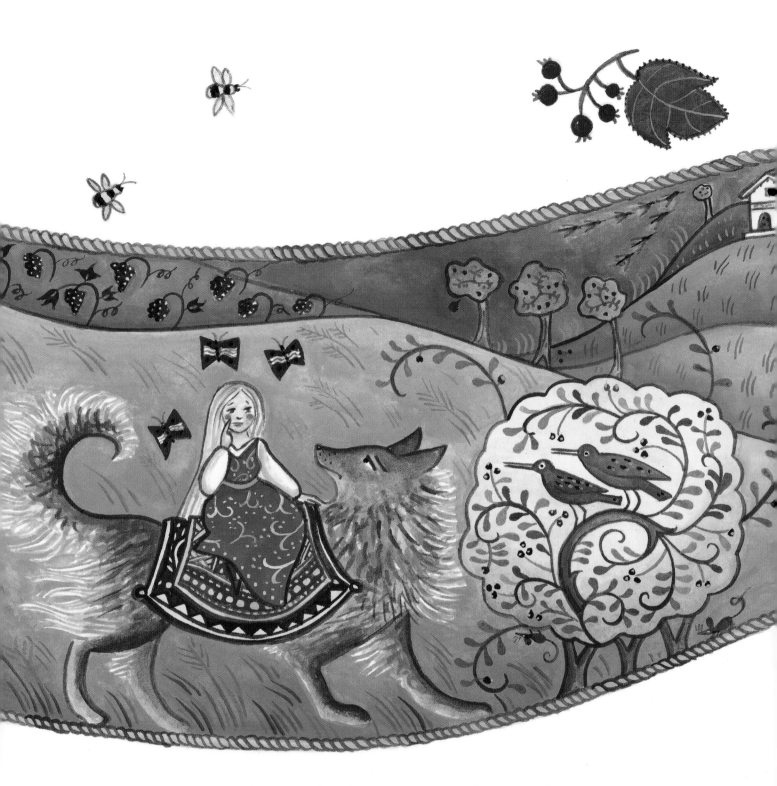

By now she was thinking of getting home to her father,
and she forgot to be kind to the dog.

"Oh, I call you a GREAT SMELLY,
SLOBBERY, SMALL-TOOTH DOG," she muttered.

"WOOOOF!"

He WHIRLED and raced back to his house.
And the girl did not get to see her father that day.

Next week he found her crying again.

"Jump onto my back.
Hold tight to my fur.
I will take you home
for a visit."

Off they bounded
over the fields . . .
to the first hedge.

"What's that you
always call me?"

She vowed to say
only sweet things
about the dog this time.

"I always call you
SWEET AS A HONEYCOMB!"

"YES!" He leaped the hedge
in a single bound,
and over the fields . . .
to the second hedge.

"What's that you always call me?"

"SWEET AS A HONEYCOMB!"

"YES!" He leaped the hedge in a single bound,
and over the fields . . . to the third hedge.

"What's that you call me?"

She could see her house in the distance.

She forgot to be kind.

"A GREAT SMELLY,
SLOBBERY,
SMALL-TOOTH . . ."

"WOOOF!"

That dog WHIRLED and flew back to his house.

Next week she was crying again.

"Climb onto my back.
I will take you
to your home."

Over the fields . . . to the first hedge.

"What's that you always call me?"

"I call you SWEET AS A HONEYCOMB."

"YES!"

Over the fields . . . to the second hedge.

"What's that you call me again?"

"SWEET AS A HONEYCOMB."

"YES!"

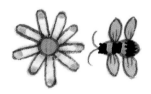

Over the fields . . . to the third hedge.

"What's that you always call me?"

And she was careful to say . . .
"SWEET AS A HONEYCOMB."

"YES!"

Over the fields and right up to her door . . .

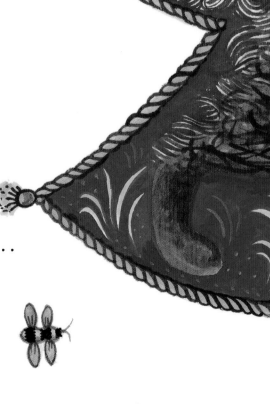

"Wait! Once more . . .
What's that you call me?"

But the girl had her
hand on the latch
to go in . . .

"A Great,
Smelly,
Slobbery,
Small-
Tooth . . ."

Then she looked
down and saw . . .
such sorrow in
that dog's eyes.

"Oh, Dog, I'm sorry.
I call you . . .

SWEET AS A HONEYCOMB.

SWEETER THAN A HONEYCOMB."

When the dog heard those dear words
and saw the look of love in her eyes . . .
he RIPPED off his smelly fur . . .

and became a HANDSOME PRINCE! . . .
with the smallest teeth you ever did see.

So she was married to the prince with the small, small teeth.

And on sunny afternoons . . .

She throws the golden ball . . . and he brings it back.
She throws the ball again . . . and he brings it back.

Then they sit in the shade of a tree,
and she strokes his hair,
which isn't smelly at all anymore,
and murmurs . . .

"Dear Prince, you are SWEET AS A HONEYCOMB . . .
SWEETER THAN A HONEYCOMB."

THE MEANING OF THE FLOWERS

THISTLE

danger and protection

CAMPANULA

gratitude

MARIGOLD
despair

OAK
bravery

THE MEANING OF THE FLOWERS

JESSAMINE

separation

RED COLUMBINE

fear and trembling

DAFFODIL
unrequited love

SWEET PEA
departure

WHEAT   *riches*

CURRANTS
you please

ROSEMARY

ANEMONE

forsaken